To: Matthew
A magical story
for a magical you

From:

Oh no!
The wizards
were in
BIG trouble!

A wicked witch had cast
an evil spell completely covering
their magical kingdom in
slimy and extremely smelly goo!
ALL of the wizards were trapped!

4

The wizards really needed
someone to help them catch
the wicked witch,
but **who?**

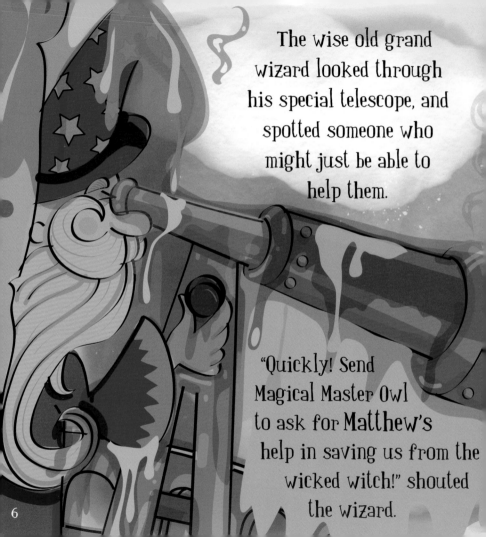

The wise old grand wizard looked through his special telescope, and spotted someone who might just be able to help them.

"Quickly! Send Magical Master Owl to ask for **Matthew's** help in saving us from the wicked witch!" shouted the wizard.

Magical Master Owl knew he had
to help so he flapped and fluttered
as swiftly as he could to find the boy
spotted through the telescope.

7

"WHIZZ BAM !"
Matthew said, as he waved his pretend wand towards his dog Ruffles.

"Oh Ruffles you are supposed to turn into a **flying dog.**"

Matthew **SO** wanted to be a Wizard.

Suddenly with a flitter and a flap, Magical Master Owl squawked through Matthew's window into the bedroom and explained (in his best owlish) the trouble the wizards were in, and asked a shocked Matthew if he could help.

9

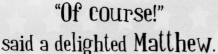

"Of course!"
said a delighted Matthew.

So Magical Master Owl squawked
three times, flapped his wings
four times, and with a WHIZZ
PUFF, a broomstick, cape and
magic wand suddenly appeared!

Matthew put on the cape,
picked up the wand,
and jumped on his brand
new broomstick.

Quick as a flash
they zoomed out of
Matthew's window to look
for the wicked witch.

11

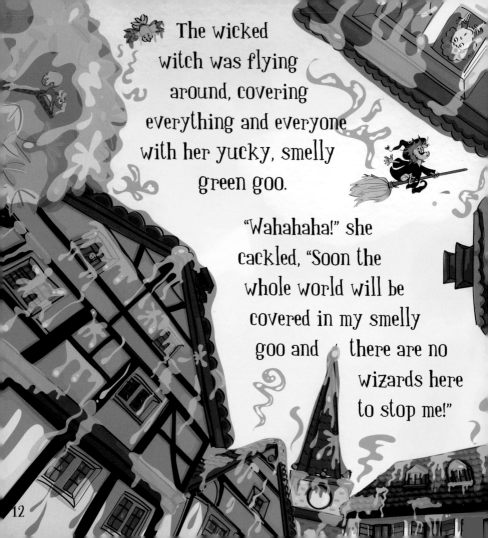

The wicked witch was flying around, covering everything and everyone with her yucky, smelly green goo.

"Wahahaha!" she cackled, "Soon the whole world will be covered in my smelly goo and there are no wizards here to stop me!"

But little did she realise that Matthew was on his way.

He zoomed under bridges...

...and over houses, looking for the goo-spreading witch.

Suddenly Ruffles made
a big booming **bark**.
His super-smelling nose had caught
a whiff of the wicked witch, but she
was too far away for Matthew
to cast a spell on her.

Matthew clicked
his heels, gripped his
broomstick even tighter,
and zoomed at supersonic speed
towards the wicked witch.

15

Finally Matthew
caught up with
the wicked witch.

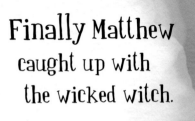

"Who are you?" the wicked
witch sneered, as she
launched a **massive** dollop
of **sticky** green
goo at Matthew.

With lightning speed
Matthew waved his magic wand.
"BIZZ POP GOO I will stop you!" he shouted.
A huge brightly-coloured umbrella appeared,
deflecting all of the smelly goo.

17

The wicked witch squealed with anger, zapping another dollop of smelly green goo towards Matthew.

"WHIZZ SPLAT send me your hat!" Matthew shouted.

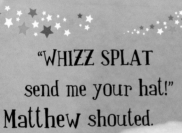

The witch's hat flew off her head, catching all of her smelly green goo. Yuck!

The witch couldn't believe what this boy wizard was doing!

"ZIP ZAP, you will be
trapped in your hat!"
Matthew cast another spell.

The witch's goo-filled hat
flew back to her,
squashing down
over her head,
squishing
her in the
smelly
green goo.

Hurray the wicked witch was trapped!

19

A triumphant Matthew took the wicked witch back to the wizards' castle.

All the slippery, slimy green goo had now gone thanks to Matthew breaking the bad witch's horrible spell.

The wizards were so grateful to
Matthew that they let him keep the cape,
broomstick AND magic wand!

Matthew finally felt like a true wizard!

The End

COLOUR ME IN

_____'S

BOOK OF SPELLS